THE BRAVE
IN ME

BROOKS CLUB

Rooted in Love,
Growing with Purpose

Written by
Michelle Beetz

**When I wake up and start my day,
I shine in my own special way.**

I roll, I hop, I zoom, I glide
I carry all my brave inside.

Sometimes I wear a patch or brace,
But strength and courage fill my face.

Some days are hard and full of tears,
But look how far I've come in years.

My hearing aids sing melodies,
My voice is loud with dreams and glee.

I may need rest or quiet time,
But watch me dream to learn and climb.

I laugh, I play,
I sometimes cry
But I keep reaching for the sky.

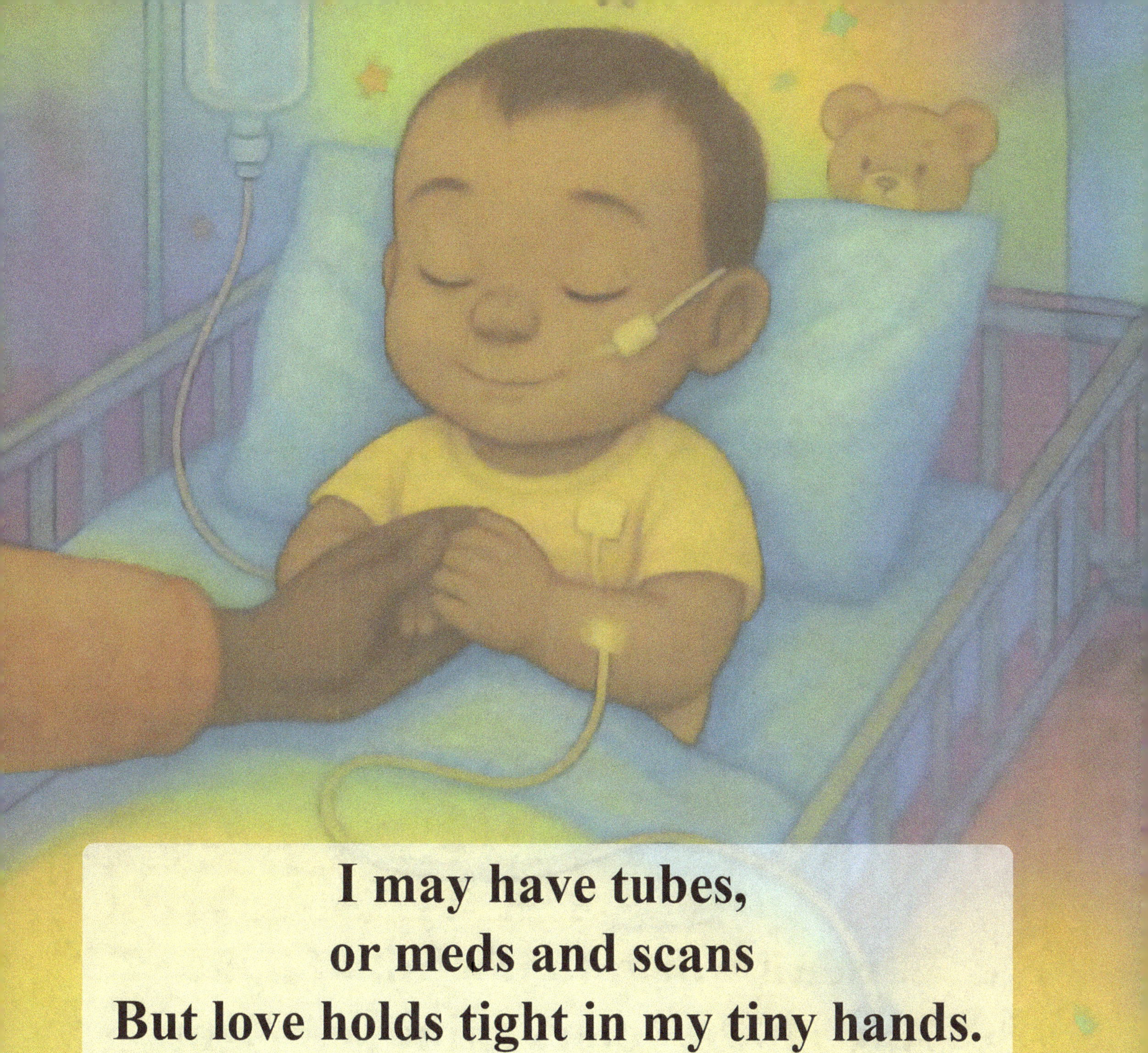

I may have tubes,
or meds and scans
But love holds tight in my tiny hands.

I see a world that's full of light
And all the colors shine so bright.

My legs may walk a different pace,
But joy still fills my every race.

My chair has wheels, it takes me far.
To playgrounds, parks, and shooting stars.

Doctors help and nurses cheer,
But heroes grow right here.

Some friends use signs or special tools,
We all belong in every school.

**Every child has songs to sing
No matter what their journey brings.**

So let's stand tall, let's all believe
In every child, in every dream.

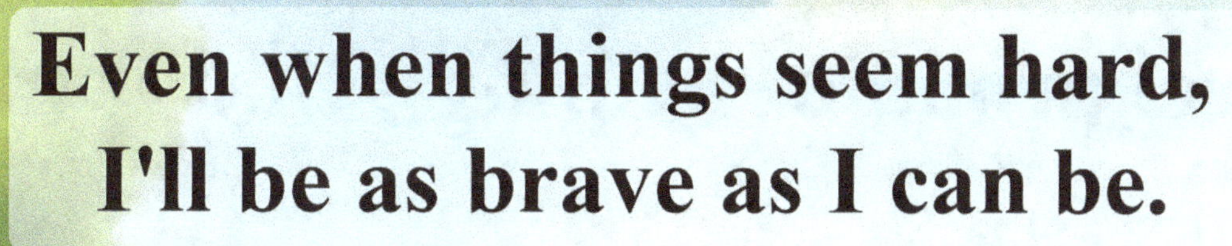

Even when things seem hard,
I'll be as brave as I can be.

The brave in me is always there,
though sometimes hard to see.
But helping others brings it out.
I feel proud of helping - that is me.

So when you see me, wave hello.
Let's be best friends and let love grow.

We're different, yes and that's just fine.
Together all our stars will shine

Because the bravest thing you'll ever be,
Is Wonderfully, Powerfully, Beautifully Me!

I am strong.
I am kind.
I am brave
inside and out.

Some bravery is loud-charging ahead, leaping high.

But some bravery is quiet-like getting out of bed,
trying again, or facing a new day with hope.

This gentle, poetic story honors the everyday courage
of children who walk through big feelings, medical
journeys, and life's unknowns with quiet strength.

For every child who's ever whispered, "I can do this,"
this book is a loving reminder:
You are brave. You are seen. You are not alone

Certificate of Bravery
This certifies that:
is part of The Brave in Me Club for
showing courage, strength, and kindness.
BROOKS
CLUB

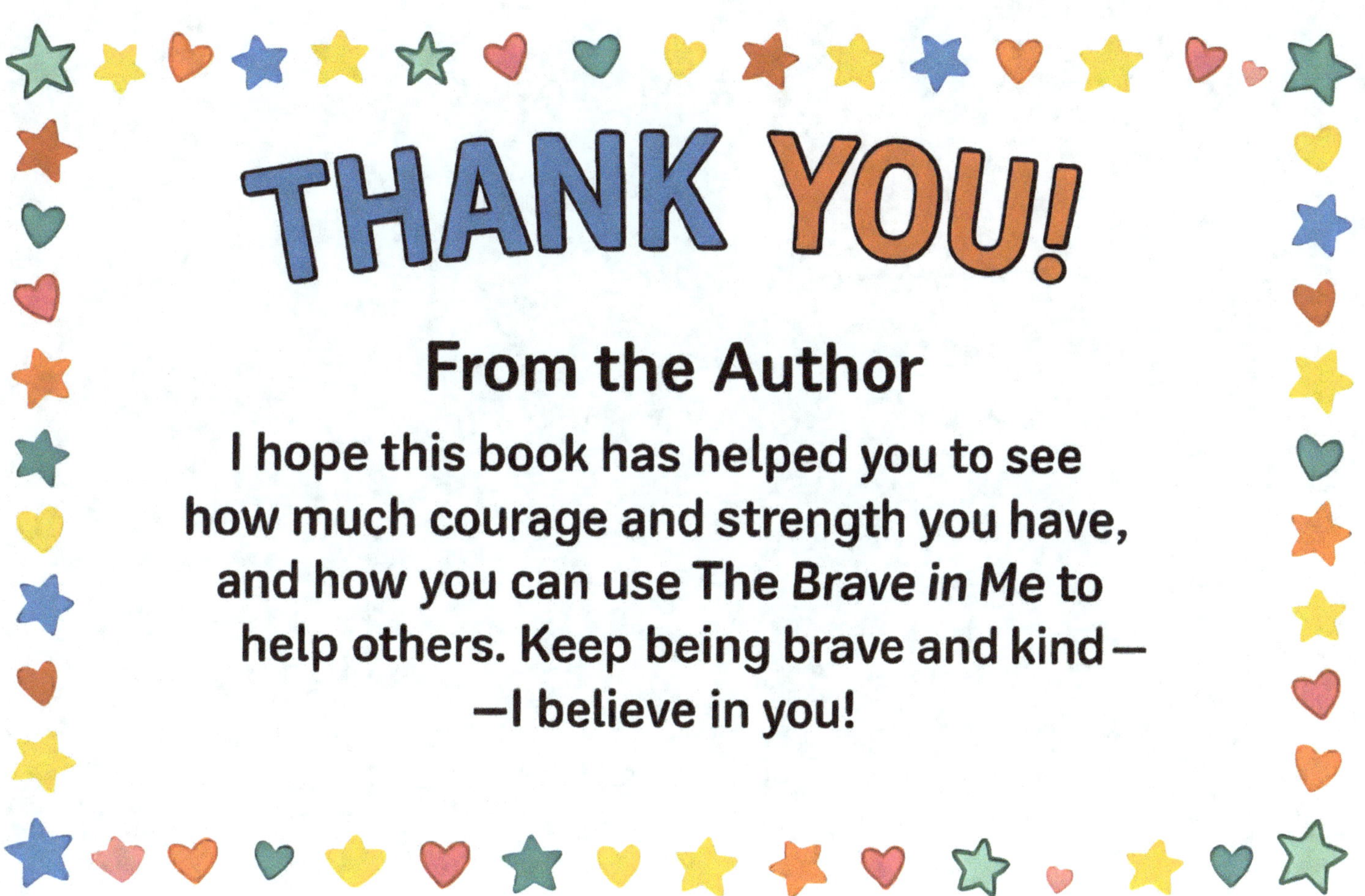

THANK YOU!

From the Author

I hope this book has helped you to see how much courage and strength you have, and how you can use The *Brave* in *Me* to help others. Keep being brave and kind—
—I believe in you!

www.ingramcontent.com/pod-product-compliance
Lightning Source LLC
Chambersburg PA
CBHW080424010826
48976CB00020B/2695